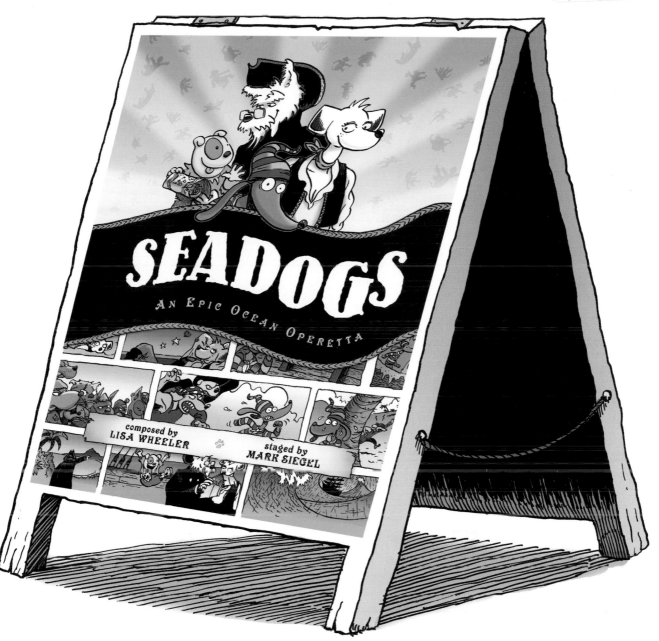

For Uncle Bill, Grandpa Oggie, and Papa Bob—seadogs, three—
and Shane, my pup
—L. W.

For you, Siena
—M. S.

A Richard Jackson Book

Atheneum Books for Young Readers

New York   London   Toronto   Sydney   Singapore

Sea Fever

Old Seadog yowls
a lonesome cry,
a homesick howl
for surf
and sky,
a yearning
he cannot deny. . . .

And all he asks
is a tall, tall ship
and a star to steer her by.

(WITH SINCEREST RESPECT FOR
JOHN MASEFIELD, 1878–1967)

"Will you sail?"
Old Seadog begs
the two hounds at his side.

The Crew

"One last sail?"
Old Seadog says.
"A rough-'n'-tumble ride?"

"Into the sea,
just we three,
if I can get ye to agree."

"Will you go? Will you go? Will you go?"
Dear Dachshund whimpers low.

"Will you sail? Will you sail? Will you sail?"
Brave Beagle wags her tail.

"WAY, HAY, WESTERLY BLOW,
TO THE SEA! TO THE SEA! TO THE SEA WE GO!"

GRANDPAW'S GROOMING

The Beauty

The BEAUTY is a bonny ship
a-sittin' in the bay,
a-waitin' for a fairer wind
till she be under way.

Then fare you well, ol' Corgytown,
fare you well, we sing.
We're off to find adventure where
a dog can be a King!

We tar her hull with pine and pitch.
We shine the bosun's bell.
We scrape off all the barnacles
'cause they don't suit her well.

Then fare you well, ol' Corgytown,
fare you well, we sing.
We're off to find adventure where
a dog can be a King!

We sand and paint the mizzenmast.
We mend the flags and sheets.
We fill her mess with hearty drink
and all the choicest meats.

Then fare you well, ol' Corgytown,
fare you well, we sing.
We're off to find adventure where
a dog can be a King!

To the Sea

"Cast the lines!
Unfurl the sails!
Lift your ears!
Uncurl your tails!"

Old Seadog shouts out from the rails.

"Trim the jib!
Hoist the main!"
The crew of two
does not complain.

Old Seadog's head of this domain.

Zephyr wind
and salty air,
ruffled fur
and tousled hair.
Their destination?
Anywhere!

Old Seadog offers up a prayer.

Brave Beagle Wasn't Always Brave....

But then she joined a scurvy crew,
cut her teeth in Timbuktu,
trained and tamed the ocean blue.
'Twas lonely years and
        longing, too,
that made Brave Beagle brave.

Brave Beagle wasn't always brave. . . .

But then she sailed the seven seas,
battled mange and tackled fleas,
brought a wolf pack to its knees.
'Twas years of fearsome
        deeds like these
that made Brave Beagle brave.

Brave Beagle wasn't always brave. . . .

But then she met a dachshund, dear,
a sweet, reluctant volunteer,
who charmed the erstwhile buccaneer.
'Twas love that taught
        her heart to fear
and made Brave Beagle brave.

The Wiener Dog

"Is it fair,"
    Dear Dachshund whines,
    "that I should do the cooking?
    I know so many other tricks
    those dogs are overlooking.
"It's always me
    they send below
    whene'er they want a nibble.
    Doggone it! I am meant for more
    than sausage links and kibble.
"I never dreamed
    of serving snacks
    out of a kitchen book.
    Curse my luck, forever stuck—
    a short, short-order cook."

Old Seadog's Song

I met her in Dublin,
a fiery red lassie,
my Saltwater Taffy,
her life was the sea.

Her language was RUFF and
her manners were brassy.
Though I loved her faithful,
she cared not for me.

For she loved the ocean,
my Saltwater Taffy.
Her home was the ROVER,
her kin was its crew.

And I couldn't chain her,
that carefree young lassie.
She stole my poor heart,
then she nipped it in two.

POM
POM
POM

Attack of the Pirates

Late one night, they came aboard,
They snuck aboard at sea,
The filthy, roving Mongrel Horde
Of Captain Jacques Fifi—
        The Terrier of the Sea, oh!
        The Terrier of the Sea.

We hid, whene'er we heard a noise,
A haunting noise at sea,
The high-pitched squeal of squeaky toys—
That heartless Jacques Fifi—
        The Terrier of the Sea, oh!
        The Terrier of the Sea.

On that night, aboard our ship,
Our stalwart ship at sea,
He barked out orders, YIP! YIP! YIP!
That scoundrel Jacques Fifi—
        The Terrier of the Sea, oh!
        The Terrier of the Sea.

He sailed off with a YAP! YAP! YAP!
A vicious YAP at sea.
He took our loot, but dropped a map . . .

That careless Jacques Fifi.
        A treasure map it be, Oh!
        A treasure map it be!

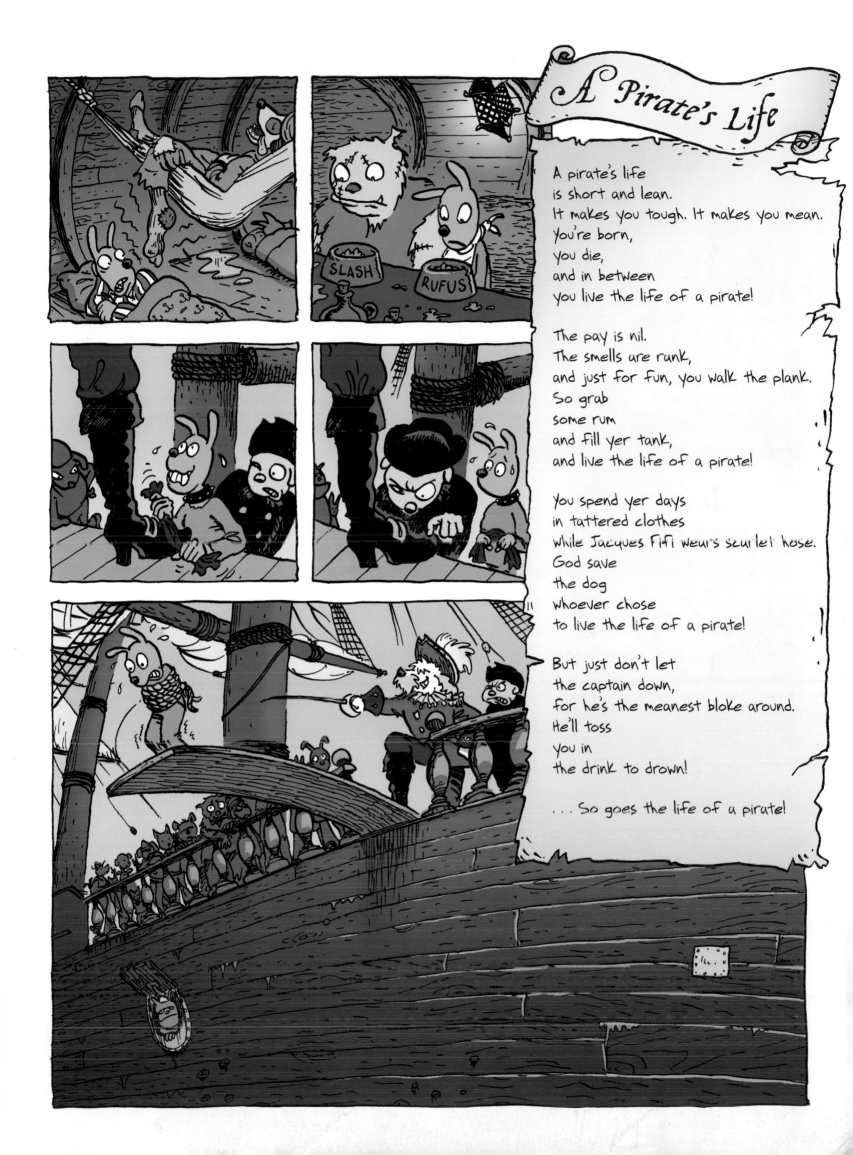

A Pirate's Life

A pirate's life
is short and lean.
It makes you tough. It makes you mean.
You're born,
you die,
and in between
you live the life of a pirate!

The pay is nil.
The smells are rank,
and just for fun, you walk the plank.
So grab
some rum
and fill yer tank,
and live the life of a pirate!

You spend yer days
in tattered clothes
while Jacques Fifi wears scarlet hose.
God save
the dog
whoever chose
to live the life of a pirate!

But just don't let
the captain down,
for he's the meanest bloke around.
He'll toss
you in
the drink to drown!

. . . So goes the life of a pirate!

The Pirate King

Said Rotty Bing
to the Pirate King,

"Our rations are meager.
The crew is quite eager
to anchor and take meat on board."

Said the Pirate King
to Rotty Bing,

"Aaarrrf . . .
'tis hard to be feeding this horde."

Said Rotty Bing
to the Pirate King,

"'Tis but a short while
till Houndstooth Isle.
Shall I tell the horde to prepare?"

Said the Pirate King
to Rotty Bing,

"Aaarrrf . . .
'tis many a bone buried there."

Fear No Fifi

The Pirate King wears fancy clothes.
A silver ring adorns his nose.
A private groomer paints his toes—
    each nail is brushed with gold.

His collar's set with precious stones.
He dabs his fur with rare colognes.
He dines on choice and savory bones
    . . . or so I have been told.

Oh, why do houndsome hearts grow faint
at pirates decked in pearls and paint?
If he's a threat, then I'm a saint
    . . . a wonder to behold!

CLAP   CLAP   CLAP

?   CLAP   CLAP   CLAP   CLAP

?   ?   CLAP   CLAP

The Stowaway

On the poop deck,
halfway hidden,
Beagle found a
wee, young pup.

"Looky here—
a cabin boy!"
She snatched his scruff
and scooped him up.

"What to do
with flea-bit beggars?
Should we toss him
in the drink?"

Old Seadog scratched
his brindled whiskers.
"This pup needs a home,
I think."

Follow the Map

Brave Beagle said,
"I'll find the isle.
My nose will lead the way."

Brave Beagle,
trusty tracker,
SNIFF-SNIFF-SNIFFED. . . .

"It's thataway!"

The Quest

The dogs set course for Houndstooth Isle,
in search of buried loot.
Old Seadog watched with wary eyes
all whilst they were en route.
He spied no terror in their wake,
no pirates in pursuit.

Soon they came to waters dark,
though silver moon shone bright,
where border collies kept patrol,
on watch both day and night.
(No need to fear, for rumors say,
they have more bark than bite.)

Dear Dachshund, faint and fearful,
hung his head and hugged the rails.
Said Seadog, wise and watchful,
"Ghost on by. I'll raise the sails."
Brave Beagle, bold and boastful,
barked, "No time to tuck our tails!"

They sailed on past the border
in a hail of howls and barks.
They sailed on past those collies
midst a swarm of hungry sharks.
They sailed on toward their destiny—
a map with crossbone marks.

Pup's Lullaby

Twinkle, twinkle
doggy star,
shining down
from up so far.

You're my watchdog
in the night.
Guard me with your
fearless light.

Twinkle, twinkle
doggy star,
keep me safe
from up so far.

The Storm

A sudden gale,
with pounding hail,
hit just beyond the coast.
Brave Beagle howled
within the storm,
but never left her post.

Raindrops lashed,
as lightning flashed,
the wind whipped cold and hard.
Dear Dachshund dropped
on trembling knees
and prayed to Saint Bernard.

Old Seadog, true,
knew what to do,
he led his crew with style.
All through the night
he chose to fight:
"Onward! Houndstooth Isle!"

The Island

Like a shadow on the water,
like a croc upon the Nile,
it lies waiting
poised and patient —
a foreboding, fateful isle.

DisemBARKING

Dogs set paws upon the sand.
Now Old Seadog takes command,
barking orders to his crew.

"**FETCH!**" RUFF! RUFF!
   "**JUMP!**" WOOF! WOOF!
"**STAY!**" ARF! ARF!
   "**SPEAK!**" AARROOOOOOOO!

As he barks, the honest pup
smiles and says, "When I grow up,
I want to be just like **YOOOOOOO**."

Old Seadog's Lament

I've never been a lap dog.
I'm old and tired and rough.
I've never wanted family.
I'm grizzled and I'm gruff.
I looked across the ocean
to see what I could see.
But there on the horizon
was me, and only me.

The ocean is my missus,
my life, my love, my all.
My spirit cried, ALL PAWS ON DECK!!
Whene'er I heard HER call.
I gave her blood and honor.
My missus served me true.
I gave her all the best of me,
and then she gave me you.

I look out to the ocean,
my missus, oh, so blue.
'Cause now on the horizon
is you, and only you.

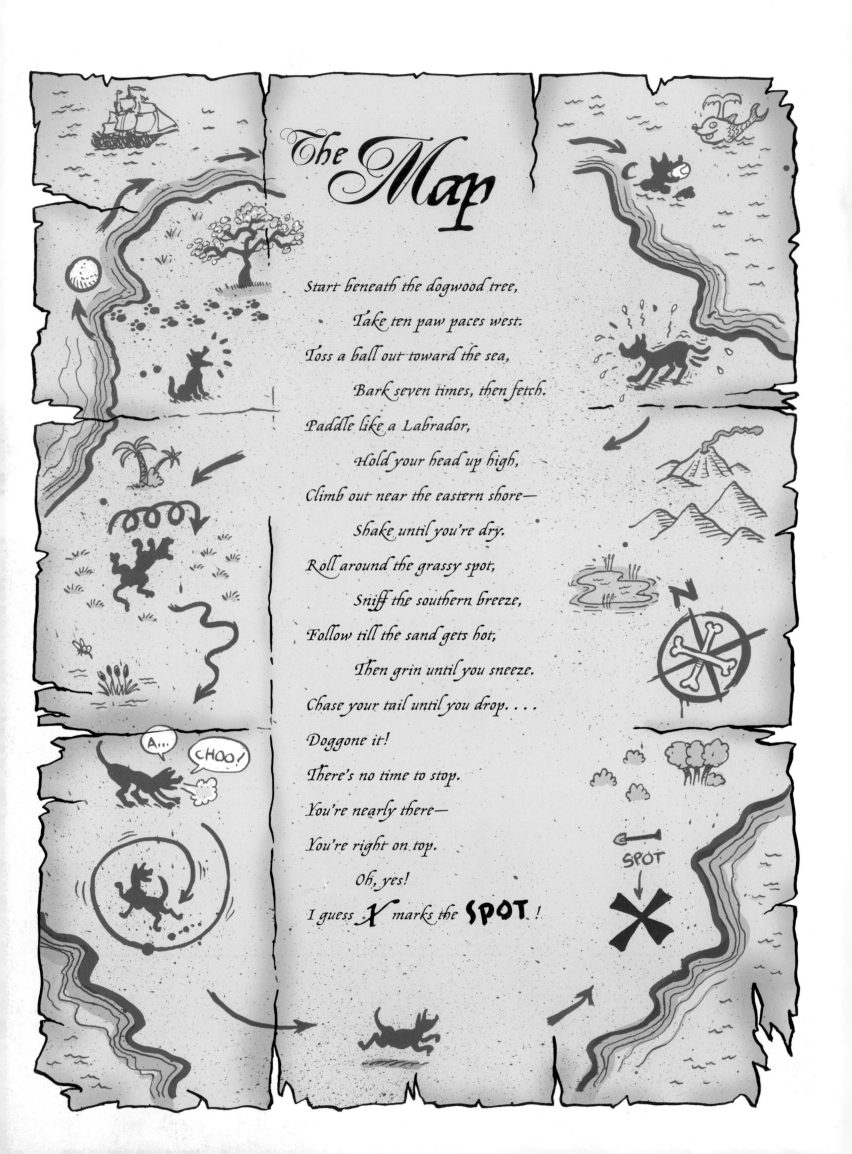

The Map

Start beneath the dogwood tree,
    Take ten paw paces west.
Toss a ball out toward the sea,
    Bark seven times, then fetch.
Paddle like a Labrador,
    Hold your head up high,
Climb out near the eastern shore—
    Shake until you're dry.
Roll around the grassy spot,
    Sniff the southern breeze,
Follow till the sand gets hot,
    Then grin until you sneeze.
Chase your tail until you drop. . . .
Doggone it!
There's no time to stop.
You're nearly there—
You're right on top.
    Oh, yes!
I guess X marks the **SPOT**!

Dig down.

Dig deep.

No rest.

No sleep.

No time

to pause,

because

your paws

will find

our cause

down

D

E

E

P

.

PING!

The Treasure

Oh! Look, look, look!
There's something there.
A box? A crate?
A chest so rare?

Haul it up. Pull it up.
H-e-a-v-e, ho!
Careful—Three more feet to go. . . .

Meanwhile, on the other side of the island . . .

The Mongrel Horde has reached dry land.
Pounding paws march on the sand.

N.C. WAGGETH

Haul it up. Pull it up.
H-e-a-v-e, ho!
That's it—Two more feet to go. . . .

The Mongrel Horde spies fresh paw tracks.
"Call the captain! Plan attacks!"

Haul it up. Pull it up.
H-e-a-v-e, ho!
Steady—one more foot to go. . . .

The Mongrel Horde tells Jacques Fifi,
"There's looters where our treasure be."

Hooray! Hooray!
The treasure's found.
Hush now, Pup,
I heard a sound. . . .

"Put up your paws!
Don't turn around. . . ."

Dogfight

Snarling, scratching
Barking, biting
Scuffling, struggling
Seadogs fighting!

Dachshund whining.
Puppy scrapping.
Seadog charging.
Beagle snapping.

Mangy mongrels
Pummeling paws
Razor teeth and
Dagger claws!

Puppy tussling.
Beagle growling.
Dachshund hiding.
Seadog howling.

"Get the treasure!"
"Grab that pup!"
"Snatch those looters!"
"Hoist 'em up!"

Beagle straining.
Puppy crying.
Seadog weary . . .

. . . Dachshund spying.

Dachsund's Dilemma

My friends have been taken.
Oh, dear.
Oh, dear.
My nerves have been shaken.
So near.
So near.
They can't be forsaken
It's clear.
It's clear.
Sweet courage, awaken—
I'm here!
I'm here!

Escape

Stealthy
seadogs
slip through night.
Pad their paws
and
douse the light.
Silently,
they steal away
to the BEAUTY
on the bay.

POW

SPLAT   SPLAT

To the Ship!

We've never seen a grander sight
nor heard a sweeter sound—
our BEAUTY bobbing in the bay,
waves splashing all around.

So weigh the anchor!
Ride the sea!
With swelling sails,
we're sailing free.

Weigh the anchor!
To the sea . . .

. . . Farewell to Jacques Fifi.

Homeward Bound

If sails and ropes
were dreams and hopes,
we'd be a merry crew.

If salt and brine
meant suppertime,
we'd have a meal to chew.

If gulls and fish
could grant each wish,
we'd never want for more.

And if the foam
should call us home,
we'll meet you on the shore, the shore . . .

. . . that heavenly distant shore.

Old Seadog's Treasure

I had no need for house nor land.
I lived my life at sea.
But Pup and me,
as you can see,
we make a family.

Brave Beagle, you shall sail my ship.
Dear Dachshund, be her crew.
'Neath Sirius
please think of us,
and we shall think of you.

And I shall keep my dear pup safe
and dry within my home.
For he's my heart,
my brand-new start.
No longer shall I roam.

This pup and me,
a family.
No longer shall I roam.

the END

Special thanks to Hilary Sycamore

Atheneum Books for Young Readers

An imprint of Simon & Schuster Children's Publishing Division

1230 Avenue of the Americas, New York, New York 10020

Book design by Mark Siegel

The text for this book is set in Printhouse.

The illustrations for this book are rendered in pen, ink, and digital color.

Manufactured in China

First Edition

2 4 6 8 10 9 7 5 3 1

CIP data for this book is available from the Library of Congress.

ISBN 0-689-85689-X